For my wife, Lou - P.K.
For Tarn - C.C.

First published in Great Britain 2017 by Egmont UK Limited
This edition published 2019 by Dean,
an imprint of Egmont UK Limited,
The Yellow Building, 1 Nicholas Road, London W11 4AN

www.egmont.co.uk

Text copyright © Paddy Kempshall 2017
Illustrations copyright © Egmont UK Limited 2017

The moral rights of the author have been asserted.

ISBN 978 0 6035 7760 4
70743/001
Printed in Malaysia

A CIP catalogue record for this title is available from the British Library.

Stay safe online.
Egmont is not responsible for content hosted by third parties.

Egmont takes its responsibility to the planet and its inhabitants very seriously.
We aim to use papers from well-managed forests run by responsible suppliers.

PETE'S MAGIC PANTS
PIRATE PERIL

PADDY KEMPSHALL ☠ CHRIS CHATTERTON

DEAN

In a wobbly old wardrobe, in the attic of Crooked Carrot Farm, a special suitcase lay hidden for many years . . .

Until Pete found it one day and discovered something wonderfully weird – the suitcase was packed with amazing MAGIC PANTS!

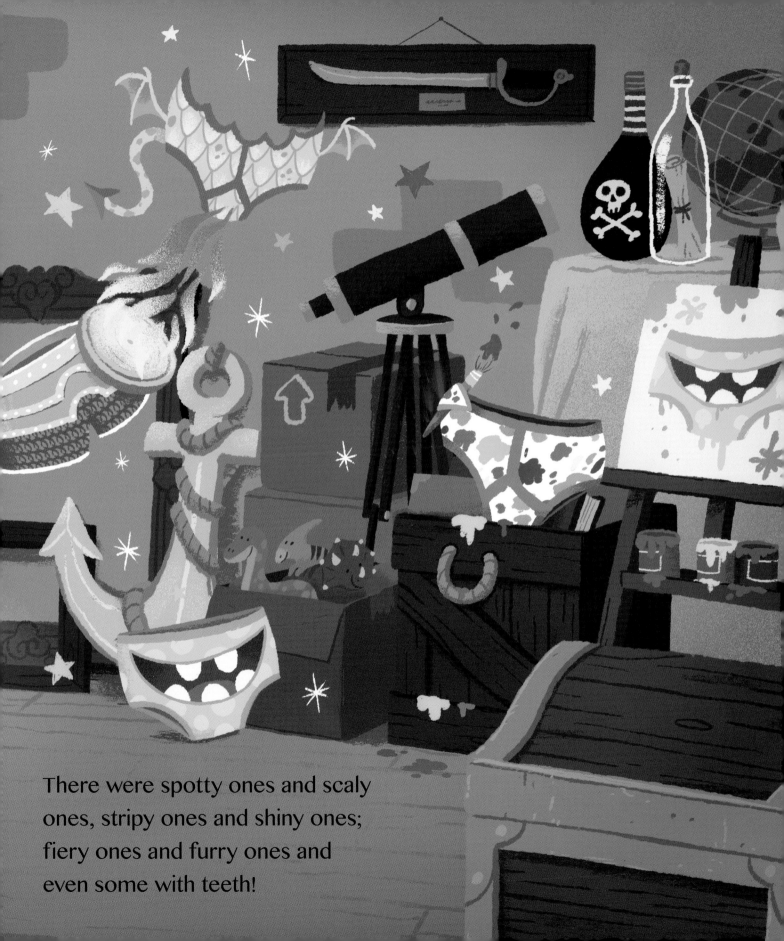

There were spotty ones and scaly
ones, stripy ones and shiny ones;
fiery ones and furry ones and
even some with teeth!

Each pair didn't just look amazing – they could also take Pete on the most incredible adventures whenever he popped them on.

"AWESOME," said Pete, scooping up a pair of pirate pants that were trying to squeeze under the attic door. "Maybe I'll find treasure . . .

Pants Away!"

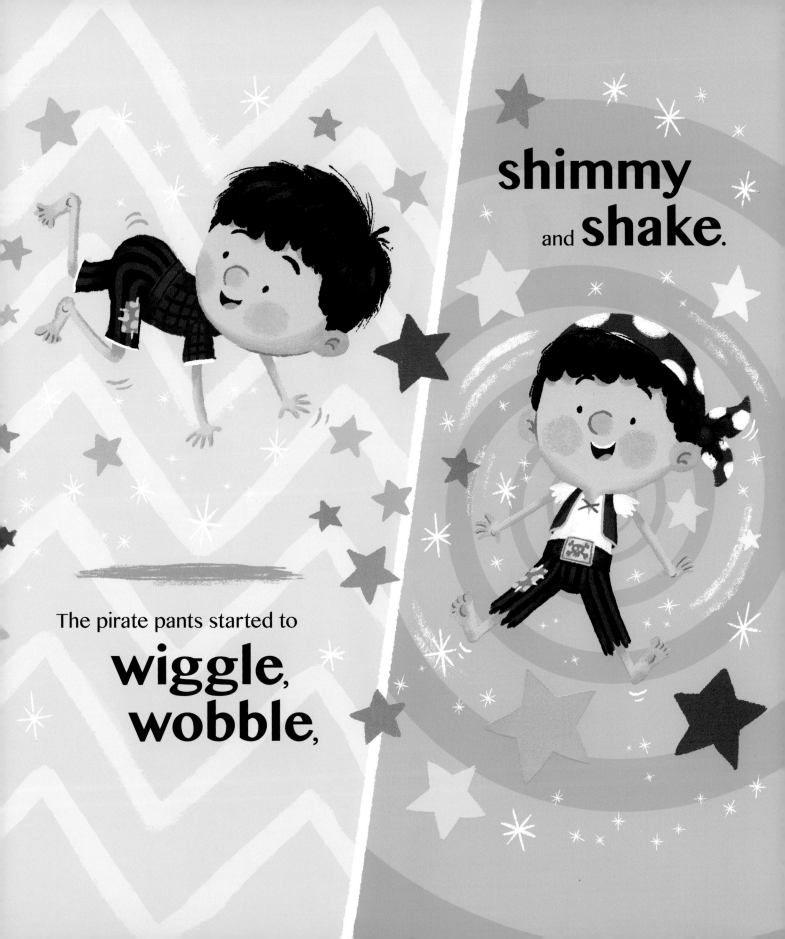

shimmy and **shake**.

The pirate pants started to **wiggle, wobble,**

Then, with a twangy ping,
Pete found himself high among
the sails of a pirate ship!

Swinging through the ropes
and down to the deck,
Pete landed nose to beak with
a small chicken wearing a big hat.

"Welcome aboard the *Flying Fowl*,"
clucked the chicken, waving a map.
"Ye couldn't help Cap'n Ted and his crew find
Long John Silverside's secret cave, could ye?
He's snaffled our treasure and hidden it there."

"**Arrrr!**" cried Pete, peering at the map.
"Um, who's Long John Silverside?"

"Ye's never heard of Long John Silverside?" squawked Ted. "He's only the smartest, tricksiest pirate on all the seven seas!"

"We'll see about that," winked Pete, grabbing the wheel. "Next stop: treasure!"

BEST PIRATE

LONG JOHN SILVERSIDE
PIRATE OF THE YEAR

But as the *Flying Fowl* cut through the waves, no one noticed a shadowy ship following just behind . . .

With a billowy wind blowing them along, the brave pirates sailed

past mischievous mermaids,

round whooshing whirlpools,

Clucking with glee, Ted steered the ship towards a spooky cave.

"Er, Cap'n," coughed Pete, pointing to the map. "Don't these squiggles look like lots of . . .

and through a shiver of sharks,

until they reached Long John's secret island at last.

... tentacles?!!"

"We be doomed! Every chick for himself!" clucked Ted in surprise, as a tumble of soggy suckers slopped over the deck and suckered up all the crew!

"Never fear, Cap'n," shouted Pete, "I'LL SAVE THEM!"

Then, ducking and dodging,
Pete grabbed his shipmates,
one by one, and tied the twitchy
tentacles into a terrible tangle!

Leaping ashore, the pirate pals
set off in search of treasure.
But the giant octopus wasn't the
only surprise on Long John's map.

There were prickly paths,

tangly nets

and even **tumbly** rocks!

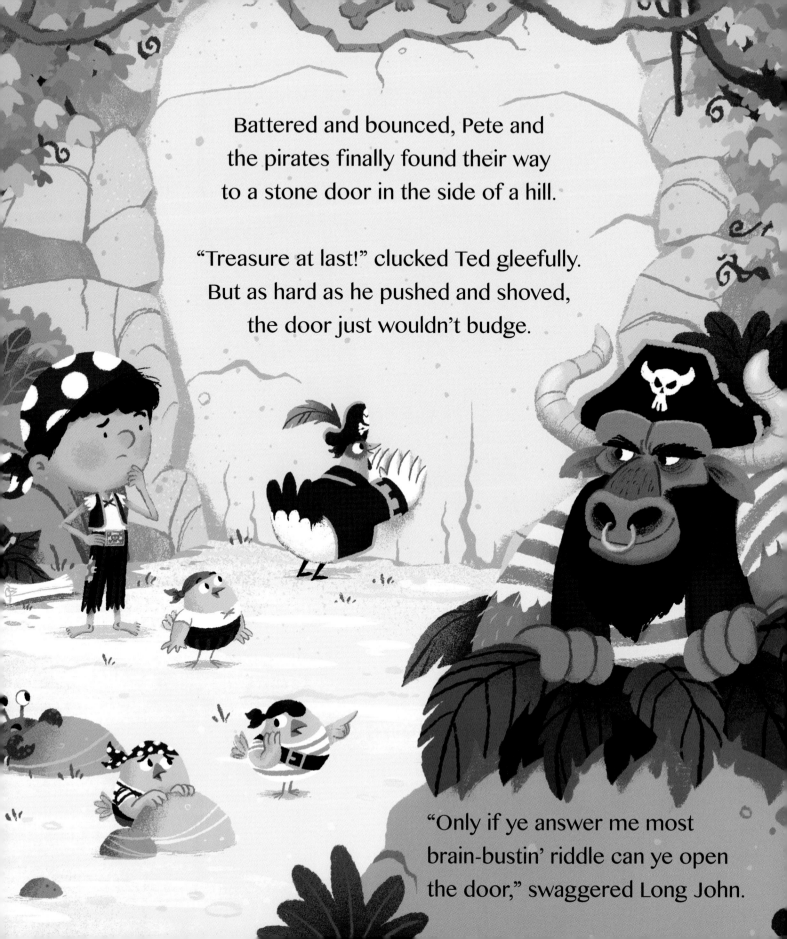

Battered and bounced, Pete and
the pirates finally found their way
to a stone door in the side of a hill.

"Treasure at last!" clucked Ted gleefully.
But as hard as he pushed and shoved,
the door just wouldn't budge.

"Only if ye answer me most
brain-bustin' riddle can ye open
the door," swaggered Long John.

Pete peered at the message scrawled in the stone:

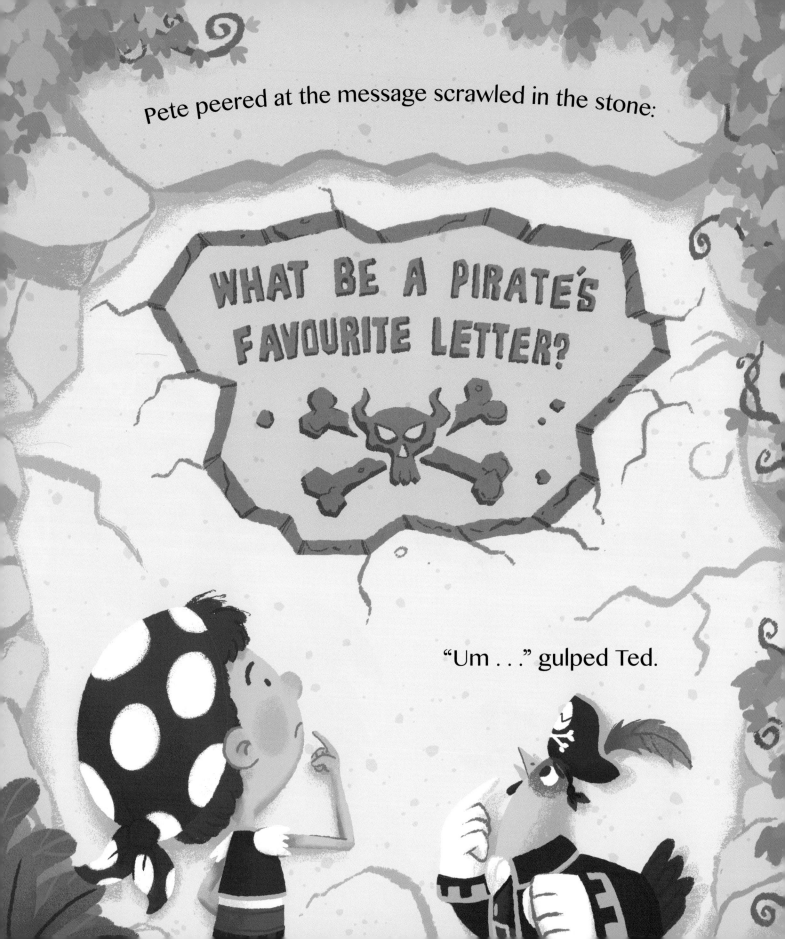

WHAT BE A PIRATE'S FAVOURITE LETTER?

"Um . . ." gulped Ted.

"Blisterin' barnacles!" cried Long John as the door rumbled open. "The lad's right!"

"TREASURE AHOY!" clucked Ted and
flapped inside to hug the huge, dusty chest.

"Not so fast," growled Long John.
"That booty belongs to me now!"

"Think again!" cried Pete, squishing
Long John's hat down over his eyes!
"Come on, Ted, let's get out of here!"

"Get back here, ye scurvy dog!" thundered
Long John, before lowering his horns and
charging with a bellowy ROAR.

But just as the fuming pirate came zooming
past, Pete hopped aside and grabbed his belt.
Then with a HUGE tug . . .

. . . he sent Long John's trousers flopping to the floor!

"I'll get ye for this!" steamed Long John, as Pete and the crew rowed away with the treasure.

Soon they were back aboard the *Flying Fowl*, surrounded by piles of glittering treasure.

"Now who be the best pirate on the seven seas?" grinned Ted. "THREE CHEERS for Pete!"

and **shimmy**
from his magic pants . . .

Then with a
shake

. . . Pete was back in the attic once more.

"**Arrrrr!**" he chuckled.
"Now that's what I call
a pirate adventure!"